GOODBYE FRIENDS

Holly Karapetkova

ROURKE PUBLISHING
www.rourkepublishing.com

See you later, alligator!

After while, crocodile!

In an hour, sunflower!

Maybe two, kangaroo!

Gotta go, buffalo!

Adios, hippos!

Chow, chow, brown cow!

See you soon, baboon!

Toodle loo, cockatoo!

Better swish, jellyfish.

Chop chop, lollipop.

Gotta run, skeleton!

Bye-bye, butterfly!

Better shake, rattlesnake.

Our school day now ends.
So, good-bye, good friends.